This edition published in 1996 by Leopard Books,
a division of Random House UK Ltd,
20 Vauxhall Bridge Road, London SW1V 2SA

The Bag of Wind first published in Great Britain in
1983 by The Bodley Head

First published in Little Greats edition 1993 by
Julia MacRae for Random House

ISBN 0 7529 0164 8

Printed in Singapore

Gerald Rose

The Bag of Wind

LITTLE GREATS

LEOPARD

Jack was a sailor. He had spent many years at sea and now he wanted to settle down. As he stepped ashore all he possessed was a Blue Macaw and a seaman's bag.

He entered the nearest tavern to quench his thirst. The landlord noticed his bulging bag and asked him what he had in it.

"Gold and silver!" screeched the Blue Macaw.

"Take no notice of the bird," said Jack. "It's only a bag of wind."

"A bag of wind!" echoed the landlord, and he laughed loudly for he had heard many such sailors' tales.

Now in the tavern there were many pairs of listening ears and one pair belonged to a particularly mean and greedy man. He sidled up to where Jack was sitting and offered him a jug of ale.

"That's a fine bulging bag you have," he said. "Could it be full of treasure?"

"Diamonds and rubies!" screeched the Blue Macaw.

"Take no notice of the bird," said Jack. "It's only a bag of wind collected from the four corners of the earth."

"But the earth has no corners and I have never heard of any seaman collecting winds," said the greedy man.

"If you choose to believe the Blue Macaw and think me a liar, then it's up to you . . ." said Jack.

"Oh, don't be offended!" said the greedy man, who was now determined to find out what was in the bag. "Come back to my house and rest your bones."

Jack accepted his invitation, and soon found himself surrounded by every comfort.

After a good night's sleep, he rose to a hearty breakfast served by the greedy man's down-trodden and over-worked wife.

While Jack spread marmalade thickly on his toast, the greedy man asked if he might just look into the bag.

"Oh no!" said Jack. "The winds would escape and, besides, there's nothing to see."

"Platinum and pearls!" screeched the Blue
Macaw.
    The greedy man ground his teeth with
impatience and asked Jack to stay another night.

The following morning while Jack was enjoying a breakfast of ham and eggs, the greedy man asked if he could just feel the weight of the bag of wind.

"Oh no," said Jack. "That would be pointless, for there is nothing to feel," and he tucked the bag even further under the table.

"Jade and sapphires!" screeched the Blue Macaw.

The greedy man gave the Blue Macaw a hard look, but forced a thin smile and invited Jack to stay a third night.

That night as usual Jack took the bag to bed with him and was soon asleep. The Blue Macaw perched on the end of his bed. The house fell silent.

Suddenly a stair creaked . . . Then a floorboard squeaked . . . It was the greedy man creeping into Jack's bedroom.

Thief and Murderer!

"Thief and murderer!" screamed the Blue Macaw.

The greedy man was so startled that he shot out of the room and down the stairs.

Jack woke up and told the Blue Macaw to be quiet. Then he turned over and dropped off to sleep again.

The next morning while Jack consumed his third kipper, the greedy man asked if he would exchange the bag of wind for his cow.

"Oh no," said Jack, for I would have nowhere to keep her!"

The greedy man thought to himself that if it was only a bag of wind, Jack would readily take the cow. He was now convinced that the Blue Macaw spoke the truth and that the bag contained untold wealth.

So after breakfast he offered Jack his barn in which to keep the cow.

"That's no good," said Jack. "What use is a barn to me without a house to live in myself?"

"Take my house as well then, if you must,"
said the greedy man, who by now was growing
desperate.

"Oh but it's much too big for me to live in by
myself," said Jack.

"I'll stay and share it with you," said the greedy
man's down-trodden and over-worked wife,
for she was tired of her husband's miserly ways.

"Done!" said Jack.
The greedy man
snatched the bag from him.

He tore at the string at
the neck of the bag, and
as he pulled there was a
strange sound . . .

At first it was a faint whistle, that became a whine, then a roar

and then an even louder roar, as all the winds from the far-flung corners of the earth tried to get out of the bag.

The greedy man was lifted off his feet . . .

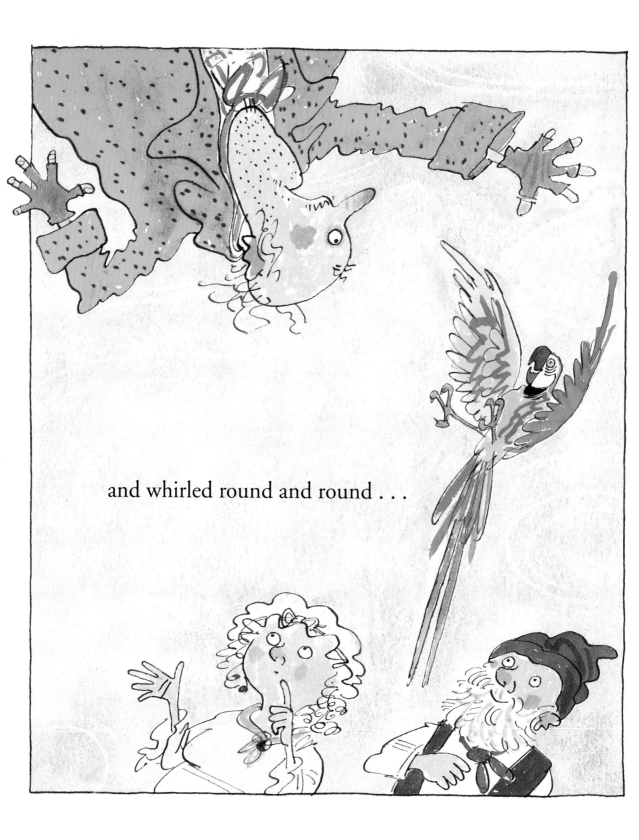

and whirled round and round . . .

over his house . . .

over the hill . . .

down into the valley . . .

and out over the sea
and he was never
seen again.